THE MISSING MITTEN ♥ MYSTERY

story and pictures by

STEVEN KELLOGG

Dial Books for Young Readers New York

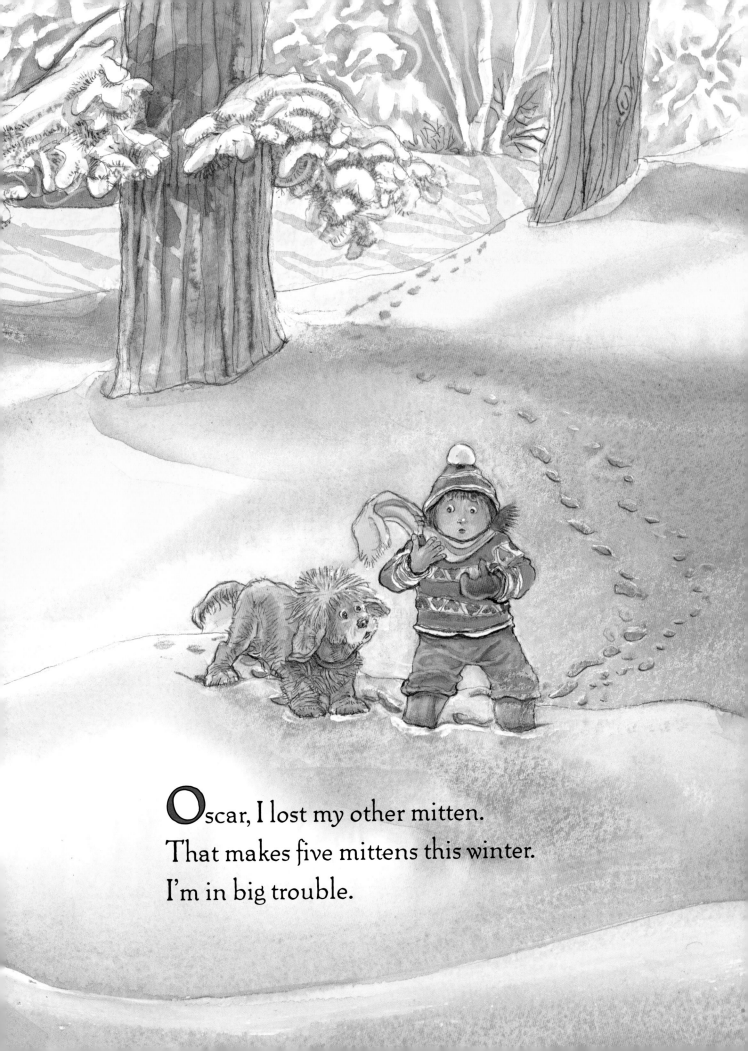

Oscar, I lost my other mitten.
That makes five mittens this winter.
I'm in big trouble.

Let's search every place we played today.
We'll start at the hill where we rode on
Ralph's sled.

Here's Ralph's boot,
but there's no mitten.

I'll look around the castles we built with

Ralph and Herbie and Ruth. That was fun!

Here's Ralph's other boot and
Ruth's sock and Herbie's sweater.

But no mitten.

Oscar!
You found it!

Wow! A flying mitten!

Oh, it's only a little bird.
I wonder if he stole my mitten
to make a snuggly nest.

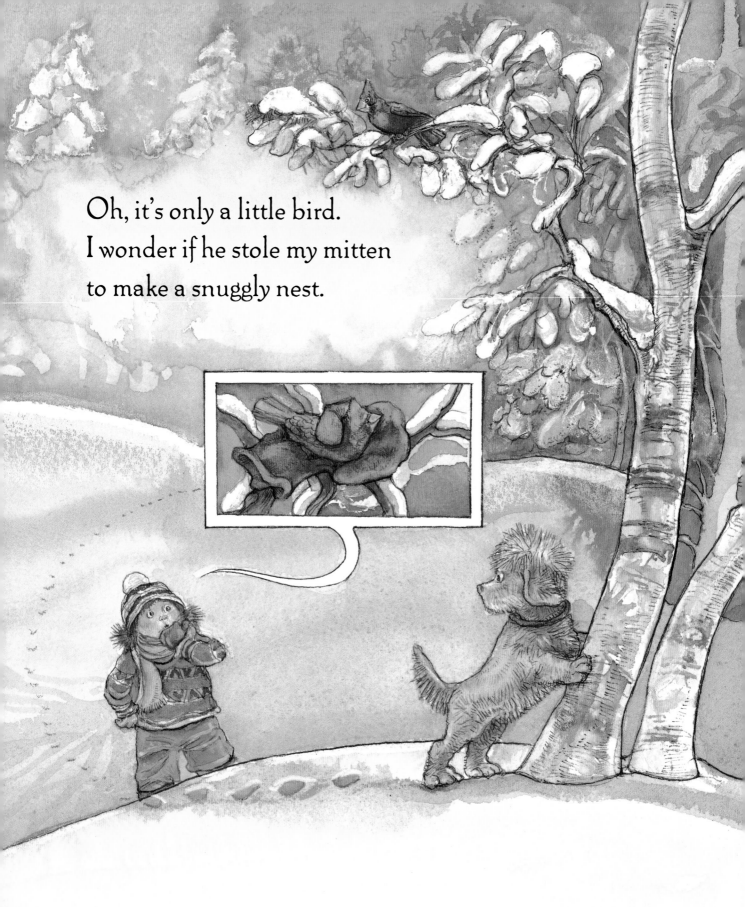

No, he's too small to carry off a mitten.

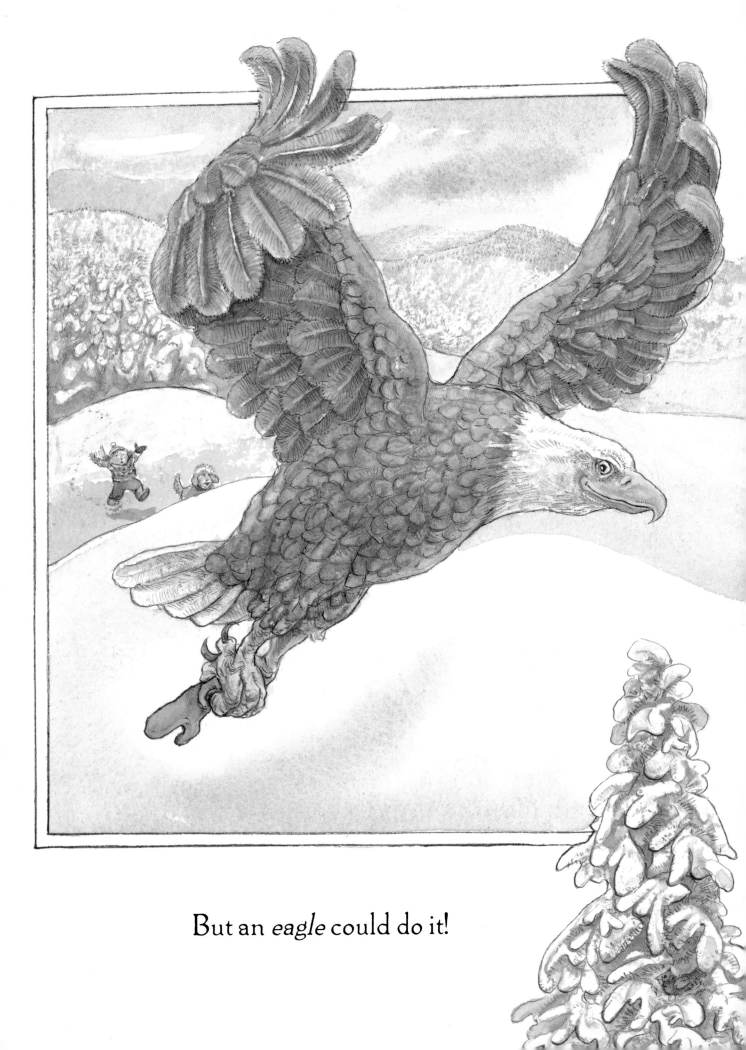

But an *eagle* could do it!

to keep his baby's head warm.

Do you think my mitten got tired of being a mitten?
Maybe it just slipped off my hand and hopped away.

There are no mitten tracks, but here are some
mouse tracks heading toward the woodpile!

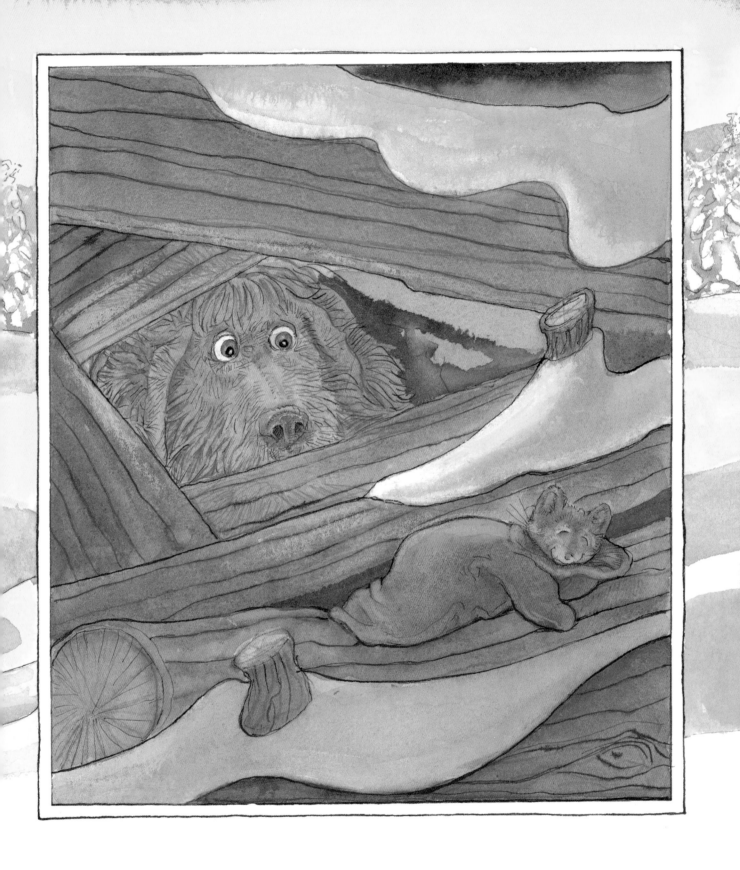

Could that mouse be using my
mitten for a sleeping bag?

Or maybe he'll wear it next Halloween
and be a mitten mummy!

Let's go see if I dropped my mitten while we were
making the snowman to surprise Miss Seltzer.

I haven't seen your mitten, Annie, but
why don't you look in the garden, where
you were making snow angels?

Finding missing mittens is hard work.
It would be easier to grow new ones!
Let's try planting the other mitten right here
in the garden. Next spring when the snow
melts, a little mitten tree might sprout.

Miss Seltzer and I would take good
care of it all summer long.

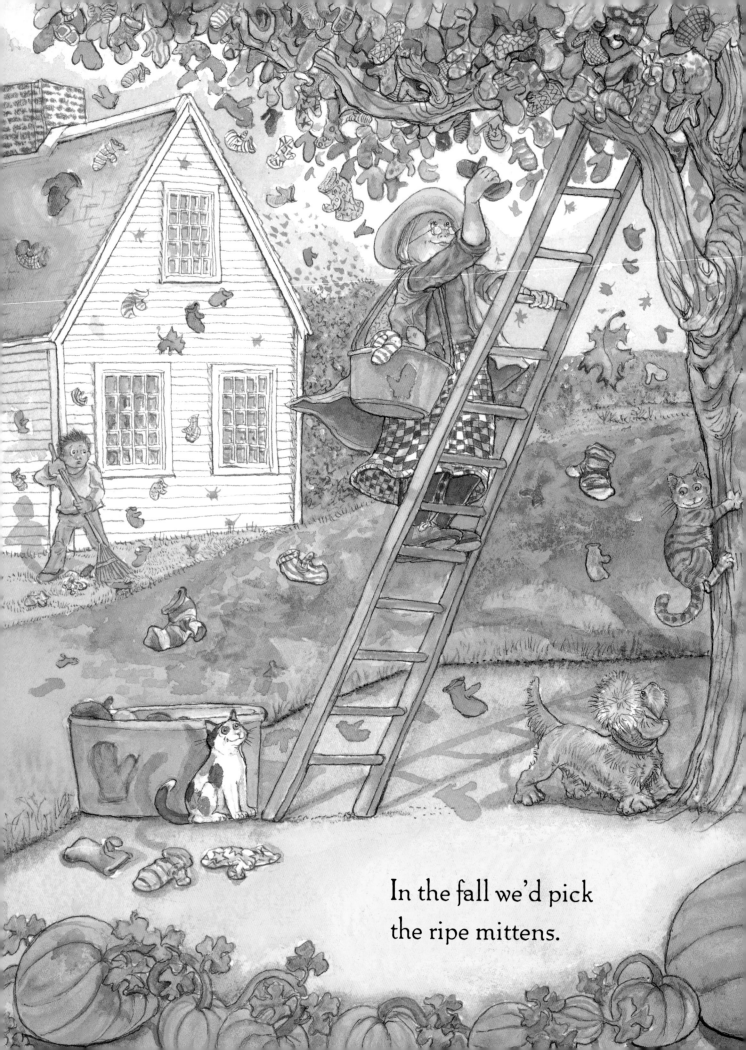

In the fall we'd pick
the ripe mittens.

Then I'd give mittens on Christmas.

And mittens on birthdays.

And mittens on Valentine's Day!

Oscar, it's getting dark and it's starting to rain.
We'll never find that mitten!

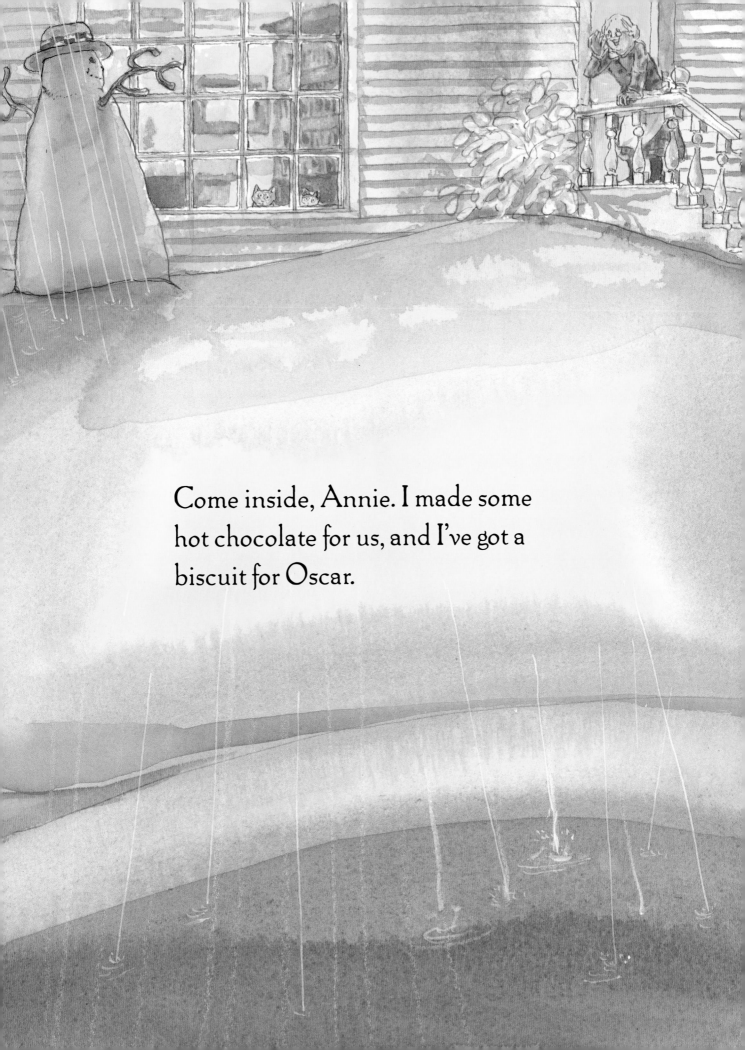

Come inside, Annie. I made some hot chocolate for us, and I've got a biscuit for Oscar.

Look! The rain is melting the snowman.
But what's that spot on his chest?

Gracious! Your snowman has a *heart*!

My mitten is the
heart of the snowman!

For Laurie with love

Published by Dial Books for Young Readers
A division of Penguin Young Readers Group
345 Hudson Street, New York, New York 10014

Copyright © 2000 by Steven Kellogg
All rights reserved
Designed by Lily Malcom
Text set in Packard
Manufactured in China on acid-free paper
9 10 8

Library of Congress Cataloging-in-Publication Data
Kellogg, Steven.
The missing mitten mystery/story and pictures by Steven Kellogg.
p.   cm.
Summary: Annie loses her fifth mitten of the winter and she
searches the whole neighborhood before she finds it.
ISBN 978-0-8037-2566-9
[1. Lost and found possessions—Fiction. 2. Mittens—Fiction.] I. Title.
PZ7.K292 Mi 2000
[E]—dc21   99-054777

The full-color artwork was prepared using ink
and pencil line and watercolor washes.